COLD JUSTICE

by

Megan Kirrmann

DORRANCE
PUBLISHING CO
EST. 1920
PITTSBURGH, PENNSYLVANIA 15238

The contents of this work, including, but not limited to, the accuracy of events, people, and places depicted; opinions expressed; permission to use previously published materials included; and any advice given or actions advocated are solely the responsibility of the author, who assumes all liability for said work and indemnifies the publisher against any claims stemming from publication of the work.

Dorrance Publishing Co
585 Alpha Drive
Pittsburgh, PA 15238
Visit our website at *www.dorrancebookstore.com*

ISBN: 978-1-6376-4269-6
eISBN: 978-1-6376-4585-7

CHAPTER ONE

Hell in a Handbasket
In Rochester, Massachusetts

Vivid images shot through my eyes, as ice cold as death itself. I saw my life vividly flash before my peripheral vision. My brother figured it was actually worth a glare when he turned around from the gun fire to discover me ominously still on the ice cold pavement. In the past, my brother's eyes would glare with the sort of cold contempt that he had towards me, as if in regret at the mere thought of having to speak with me. Almost as if through that action proved it was too unbearable to deal with me during our entire childhood.

Shockingly, it's as if his cold contempt for me was now gone without a trace, and all that remains now is his obvious concern for the life of his sister, Rex. Whether I will live tonight… only time could tell.

Trevor realized that his one and only sister had suffered severe wounds by our sworn enemy. This knowledge hit him with the harsh reality that I might not live through this bloody fight tonight.

My brother, shocked, quickly hurried to my side amidst the rapid spray of deadly bullets. "Bang…Bang…Bang" rang the gunshots my brother rapidly let loose at our sworn enemy, so he could finally reach me… alive. The Russo siblings were dressed all in black, but their true intimidation was held in their superior use of close combat. He missed our enemies by mere inches. Other bullets ricochet off of various inanimate objects.

"Are you all right, Rex?" asked my brother with panicked concern.

"Well, how the hell does it look like I'm doing…seriously?" I could have killed him for the stupid remark. Obviously, everything was not all right, and far from ever being completely over. Peering down at the gunshot wound that was inflicted upon me, I noticed one important item…BLOOD. Oozing out with dark red pools from the devastatingly painful exit wound area. The flesh wound was only a mere illusion of the catastrophic damage from the severity of the gun shot wound. It looked as if hamburger meat was trying to protrude from the mangled flesh that surrounded the entrance wound but the BLOOD expelled from the exit wound was the actual issue. As my vision blurred, my eyes faded into the pitch black of the unknown. IF serenity was found in the abyss…I truly missed it. (My recovery process discovered in Chapter 3 in the hospital from the gunshot wound would all be divulged later after my past tragedies and training thereafter…)

I would soon dream of the nightmares from my past horrors vividly. Recurring nightmares are always the scariest when the nightmare is a mere real life tragic event. MY horrors came back to haunt me. I slowly began to re-live my childhood in my fading subconscious mind.

———— A Decade Ago…————

There was a specific day I could remember when I was sixteen years old. It was July 4th, 2000 at 5:30 P.M. The actual holiday that would change our lives forever…I remember gathering plates and silverware around for our annual family dinner. I had not a single clue as to what would happen in the few moments to come. Events that would not only un-nerve the very foundation of my central core being but move forward a vindictive need for justice and family honor. I never had any previous life experiences that would require me to later seek out justice and then vindication. I began naively humming to myself in the kitchen. Everything was fine, the perfect day for a family to get together. Or naively thought…

So, after Mom had prepared the meal of grilled steak seared to perfection with raspberry and lemon homemade sherbet ice cream for dessert, I finished all the dinnerware and plate setting, understanding what my mother had taught me. A few moments later, juicy and savory meats with caramelized onions were smelled, fresh off the grill. Their scents wafted through the summer heat, making for an even greater experience. My mother was one of the best cooks around; everyone agreed in tonight's family get together conversation. Our family naively thought it was just another fun-filled family get together for the holiday season. Soon, our family would quickly realize that a quiet family night was not quite what was in store tonight. Destroyers of all that is decent and humane were prowling outside our home in the dusk hour precluding to nightfall. To avoid attention from the neighbors, they took the utmost care in their swift and stealthy approach. Now, with steadfast determination, they had secretly crept up our front stairs to take a quick peek into our home.

"How was band camp at the senior high school retreat, Trevor? I heard you have a new instructor this year? Tell me all about your new—"

Gunshot blasts quickly ignited the air with a deafening sound. Gun smoke immediately had an overwhelming smell that seemed to engulf the room. The first bullet in the air went directly straight through my mother's forehead with a sickening wet sploosh sound. A splatter of her own BLOOD lightly sprayed across the right side of my face. White walls were completely surrounding the kitchen, but now the back wall that was white changed drastically to a stained crimson from my own mother's precious blood. Lightly touching the right side of my face, I peered down at my fingers to view my own mothers blood slightly resting on my finger tips. Without hesitation, I let out a blood-curdling scream of anguish. Raw emotions of hatred took over my entire being, with the realization that my mother had recently been horrifically murdered right in front of me.

The second gun shot blast hit my father straight through his hand. "Damn it!" he screamed out in agonizing pain as he stood up from his chair and flung his seat towards the left side of the white kitchen. It felt as if everything was turning into complete chaos rather quickly, when only a few minutes previously our family had been in serene tranquility prior to the intruders having invaded our home. Intruding on our family's sacred peace by introducing unwanted chaos into our home was unforgiveable.

I do mean UNWANTED to the fullest extent of the word.

Luckily, another bullet went right through one of the drinking glasses at the table, I saw it shatter into a hundred pieces. I always thought of our home as a haven. That's what I believed....

Already injured, my father literally leapt across the room towards the small, yet very stocky intruder. I watched as my father tackled the stocky man dressed all in black. Later I would realize that my mood could match that exact outfit...just as black...but I would carry it all in my heart. A BLOOD curdling scream erupted from the stocky built man as my father applied enough pressure to snap two of his fingers with white bones showing through his mangled flesh. In a fit of rage, the intruder took his other hand (anguish written in his voice),
"This pain is so intense, I can't take much more of this!!"
And with one meaty, full-functioning hand, grabbed my father. He threw my father across the room and bounded on top of him. "No!!" I screamed out and quickly lurched proactively to save my own father. Missing my target, I tripped and fell on the evil man, knocking the wind out of his chest.
Quickly, before I even realized, my hands were viciously scratching at the intruder's face and eyes sockets. Small traces of blood exuded up from the various scratches I inflicted upon him. In mere seconds after that, I was being menacingly strangled by the intruder. Seconds later, my vision began to get blurry and then....My brother Trevor screamed in the distance....
Then everything I envisioned seemed to ebb into the pitch black abyss. I would soon realize that this horrific event would not only take over my future way of life, but my very own vulnerable soul.

 ——— Hours Later ———

"Wake up Rex, Damn it!! I need you alive...you're all I have left in this world. Damn it!!"

Cold splashes of liquid quickly fell onto my face.

"Wh- Wh- What the hell?" I gasped in between taking a deep breath of water straight down my esophagus. "We should be on the run since the intruders know where we live…What if there are others?" A freaked out Trevor exclaimed.

"Why do we have to hide from them…Where the hell are the intruders located now?" I asked Trevor, rubbing the bruise on my neck.

"I honestly don't know," said a stupefied Trevor.

"Sounds great to me, Trevor," I sarcastically retorted. Suddenly, I saw slowly making its way toward me…BLOOD and a lot of it!!!! Where was it coming from exactly? I wondered to myself…then I finally got up to examine both our parents were dead as door nails. One door nail that I would love to ram rod straight through the intruder's head; *Straight through their wretched skulls*, I thought sadistically to my own horrified self. "Sorry, I feel really disoriented," I quietly mumbled to Trevor. "Wait, let me help you up from the floor Rex," my brother quickly said after he swiftly picked me up off the floor.

Looking down, I quickly realized how my father met the end of his fate, through several stab wounds aimed precisely towards his carotid arteries. His neck and entire torso were such a grotesque mess, that it was hard to even identify him. There was so much BLOOD pooled up around him that it looked as if he was swimming in it…literally. I let out a BLOOD curdling scream of anguish and remorse at the devastatingly actual hard truth.…My father now is truly gone from this earth. A man with no story to tell, and my own mother, a scared woman just caught in the bloody aftermath of violence.

"Rex, snap out of it. Pay attention to what I am about to say," said Trevor adamantly.

"All right Rex," Trevor began as he leaned into my face only mere inches away from the tip of my petite turned up nose, "We… totally vanished… So "they" can't come back to kill us."

"They? Who the hell are "They?" We don't even know who they are… they're complete strangers!" I asked Trevor in my emotional exhaustion.

"Duh, 'they' are the intruders that came into our home and brutally killed our parents, if you were even thinking clearly…" said an exasperated Trevor as he rolled his eyes at me.

"Who the hell do you think you are? Don't you dare roll your eyes at me…" I could not control my emotions any longer. Viciously, I slapped him across the face, leaving my hand impression still plastered across his shocked face.

"Calm down sis, he held up his hands in self defense, we have to slow it down. You're right, there is no reason for us to lash out at each other. Now, let's take the next step in our plan."

"What exactly is the next step?" I asked coolly.

"Getting the hell out of here! This area is a crime scene! It's not safe for anyone!!"

"Where the hell are we going, then?" I asked. *God he's an IDIOT!!!* I quietly thought to myself, *he's going to get us BOTH killed.*

"Am I being too dramatic?" I questioned myself. I gave myself a break. After the harsh realization hit me that my parents USED to be alive, but now they were nothing more than dead, limp, lifeless cadavers awaiting their next burial plot in the cemetery. The sad realization where no one would truly know who or why they had been brutally murdered... I wept. Tears of remorse, tears of injustice, and overall frustration at needing a complete understanding as to why this occurred.

A murderous face that was unidentifiable... justice must be served.

Previously waking up confused, my strange feelings and emotions still remained with me, like an unwanted thorn in my side.

"Where the hell are those intruders?" I screamed in hostile angst.

Trevor pointed with a crimson face filled with rage as he glanced at what was painted on the door.

The BLOOD drenched letters, disturbingly written on the back door read: BACK SOON...and when curiosity got the best of me, I hastily swung the door open to notice the other side of the door creepily announced...STILL HERE.

Our blood-curdling screams; due to the BLOOD drenched writing on the door, immediately emanated out into the pitch black sky above.

Panic quickly pumped through my veins, giving me some much needed adrenaline as I grabbed the phone with a trembling hand to make a quick call to our local police department. Seconds after the phone call, as that one side of the door said STILL HERE...

I ripped the emergency contact information off the wall where it had been taped right beside the phone. Our parents always told us that whoever was at the top of the list should be contacted immediately. One name edged its way to the top... Arnold Hamilton. An old military friend of my father's, but we had not been in contact with him in almost two years. Well, we were about to make contact with Arnold now. Quickly, I hastily made the call and explained our predicament. Arnold gave strict directions to his house, since we had never been there. All he said after that was "The intruders left a sign that announced STILL HERE? You kids better announce your departure from that house... PRONTO!!" and with that said he quickly hung up the phone.

A decent sixty seconds later, we were both out the door with the basic essentials we needed to survive. Where would we go? Who would help us eventually stop these intruders? Would the brutal murder of our own parents ever finally be brought to justice? How could we desert the only safe haven we knew all these years...for the mysterious and unforgiving world of the unknown?

CHAPTER TWO

On the Run...Training Days...

After twenty minutes of running, Trevor and I finally arrived at the bus station. Patiently waiting, the bus arrived around five minutes after we sat down. We hopped on the bus and made our way towards Marlborough, Massachusetts, where our ex-Marine friend of the family was living. The heavily wooded area made the perfect location to temporarily go undetected by those brutal intruders that ruined our entire lives in just a matter of a few hours. They would later become extremely challenging. Not only were they experts at hand-to-hand combat, but they also carried high levels of intelligence on various deadly weapons. The journey to our destination took roughly two hours, with several intermediate stops along the way. It was a beautiful trip, given the circumstance, but Trevor and I had torn and frayed nerves, one too many for sightseeing. We passed Sudbury corners and Longfellow's Wayside Inn.

Finally, when we arrived in the colonial town of Marlborough, we decided to hike with our backpacks. We walked the rest of the journey. Hiking towards our true destination took around half an hour. I became suddenly aware of becoming extremely hungry and thirsty. We were in a densely wooded area. High above, you could just get a glimpse from the tops of the various evergreen trees. Off in the distance, you could witness a predatory peregrine falcon swoop down and fly off with a snake wrapped protectively in its closed talons. Underneath our feet were various pine cones, pine needles, evergreen pieces, and black dirt with worms wriggling in and out of it, fighting for survival... we were the same as those worms.

"The forest of no return... Just look around us..." I replied with an ominous tone.

About fifteen paces ahead, located directly in front of us, was a barn building that would later serve as our training facility. House on a plateau where you could barely notice it within the densely crowded forest surrounding the house. A quiet Sunday after church would match with the exact setting where we would be training. Still, no Sunday morning at church would be acquired during our specific brutally mastered on site training. Trevor gave a heavy-handed knock on the door of the white framed house just beyond the barn. A few moments later, Arnold opened the door.... "Jesus, what are you doing? Come on in! I heard the news about your parents!"... we both wept.

After explaining to Arnold Hamilton what happened at our house, we both felt emotionally drained and exhausted. Quickly, gathering us close together, he gave us a strong embrace while one single bitter tear of his own ran down his extremely saddened countenance.

"Semper Fi," said Trevor through his own bitter tears. "We need to stop for a second here."

"Hell yes, you must be hungry. Get on in here." Arnold Hamilton commanded, since he was after all, a Marine.

Now retired, he teaches karate classes and the safety practices of proper weapon usage and is an old school farmer, do you consider that retirement? Anyways, he was best friends with our father. He was an ex-Marine that served with my father in the Vietnam War. They met during the war and survived and were best friends ever since that time. After the war, the correspondence was only through the postal mail services, but later turned into hanging out for about a week of camping once a month. They would end up reminiscing about all events past and present.

"Rex and Trevor, damn nice to see you're both alive," he said with great enthusiasm.

"Welcome to my humble abode," he led us into the kitchen from the door.

"We want to train with you to fight the sadistic villains who murdered our parents...." Trevor said menacingly as he shook hands with the ex-Marine.

"Not a problem, glad to be of service for both of you, obviously, given your situation," as Arnold replied.

"Well, I am no wimp myself, whatever your views may be on women in combat," I said matter-of-factly as I also walked inside and shook his hand.

"Ha!" he gave a chuckle, "I wouldn't DARE mess with a woman on a mission," he gruffly stated. He softly clicked his tongue and said, "After three wives, I definitely learned my fair share of combat from them... .TRUST ME!!" he said.

We rolled our eyes simultaneously.

"All right, folks, let me show you both to your guest bedroom," he stated as he quickly went up the stairs. We followed, and to our delight found...Absolutely nothing. Minimalism must have seriously DIED in this specific room. There were bunk style-twin beds off in the right-hand corner of the room. An elaborate rug adorned with autumnal leaves was in the center of the room. In the left-hand corner was a table and two chairs. An adjoining bathroom resided by one of the chairs. A window on the other side of the room was filtering in some light into the almost vacant living space. We both put our backpacks on the table.

"Ok," I said fairly through clenched teeth.

"I'm going to fetch your dinner," said Arnold brusquely.

Trevor gave me a look as if daring me to continue with THAT sentence. I quickly considered how bad that idea would be, and just completely shut my vocal cords down to nothing.

A few minutes later, Arnold arrived with dinner for all of us. Pushing our backpacks off the table, we hurriedly made room for our highly anticipated meal. Setting a plate down for both Trevor and myself, we could only stare in amazement. Before us lay steak grilled to perfection with carmelized onions... just what our mother had made for us on the same day... the day our lives changed forever.

"Food is getting cold, come on, everyone dig in!" he said putting on a cheerful tone of voice to soothe recently frayed nerves from the aftermath of our previous encounter with the intruders. We ate in silence, while Arnold watched us, slightly amused at our ravenous appetite. After dinner, he cleared away plates and announced:

"All right, you will rise precisely at 6 A.M. tomorrow morning to begin your training."

"Rest up kids, cause you will need to, I guarantee that," he said in an ominous tone of voice as he quickly left the room and quietly shut the door behind him.

Quickly, we both put our backpacks on the table and then proceeded to go to sleep. When an ex-Marine warns you once that there is hard work proceeding into the next day, you might have a tendency to actually listen to that individual where sleep would be involved.

The Next Day, we were woken up at exactly 6 A.M. to the sound of a blaring alarm system he held within his hand. We were given only five minutes to get dressed and ready to go. Once we were led outside, he took us towards a trail in the densely wooded area beside his house. Leading the way, we ran behind him for one mile and stopped to rest for one minute when he suddenly yelled,

"All right, folks, on to the next course in the training...pushups and sit ups!!!" he almost smiled a bit as he said it. He made us complete 100 pushups and 100 sit ups in five minutes each for both, but not combined. Keeping up with him was near impossible, but we had to keep up or we had to repeat it all if we lagged one second behind the five-minute interval to complete the exercise. After that was done, we went on to some rock climbing. Approximately twenty to thirty meters high, with no securing devices or anything. Just Arnold leading us up, but careful to instruct us where the placement of our hands and feet should be ahead of time. No nasty cuts, abrasions, or falls from ten... now fifteen meters high...I had to look up at all times for fear that I would quickly look down and then somehow end up splattered amongst the various jagged rocks below us all... DAMN.

It always seemed as if he was ten paces ahead of us, but that was just mentally...and obviously, physically from his extensive Marine training. After we reached the top of the cliff, we were allowed to rest for one minute. Without warning, Trevor was thrown onto the ground by a swift kick from Arnold. His kick was shallow enough to not cause bodily harm, but swift enough to send him hurtling to the ground.

"What the hell?" asked Trevor in complete shock over what Arnold had recently executed.

"Use that anger, Trevor, I am about to prepare you for some hand-to-hand combat training," he said as he beckoned with his hand towards Trevor in a taunting mannerism.

Overall, the martial arts training was a mix between taekwondo, jujitsu, and a little bit of kung-Fu all combined into one royal brilliance that would send any attacker crying back home to their mother's house. Crying like a bitch, is the technical terminology he used if I remember correctly.

——— Class Act ———

Temporarily feeling fatigue, I dug into my lowest reserves of energy and carried on. Trevor and I were learning now the basics of sparring with each other. After giving a slide swipe with my right leg that knocked Trevor right off his feet, the sound of his fall was deafening. Quickly, I stood up to access his overall damage.

"All right, let's see if you can handle round two," I said with a bit of a mocking undertone.

"Bring it on," said Trevor with a beckoning hand gesture. I tried attacking with a swift round house kick but Trevor cunningly caught my foot in mid-air and simultaneously slammed me down to ground level.

Yeah, thanks to egotism, that did not go very well for me. No bruised rib or side of the abdomen, just an overall bruised ego. After sparring was over, which I was excellent at (minus Trevor's swift maneuver), we went into proper usage of a 45mm pistol. Unfortunately, the weapon aspect of the training program was not something that I was excellent at...not even in the slightest. Target practice was fun, but I was too competitive and fiercely wanted to beat Trevor. He made us practice until we both received a bull's eye in the dead center of the target practice shooting sheet. Unfortunately, Trevor got his first, and then I completed mine...around half an hour later.

——— One Year Later ———

After the completion of our testing, we all sat around the dining table to celebrate our achievement with an ENORMOUS dinner. It may have not been gourmet, but it was really something worth appreciating. Spread around the table were various appetizers of meats and cheeses, following some fine raspberry Moscato wine glasses poured in front of us. Dead center in the middle of the table was a self-prepared, cooked to perfection, sugar cured spiral ham. On the other side was dessert, which consisted of one choice of three items: tiramisu, turtle cheesecake, or make your own sundae. It was more than we could ever ask from anyone.

"All right, don't just stare at it, Rex and Trevor, eat some of this amazing food!!!" he said with extreme enthusiasm shown in his voice. With a sensational appetite, we ate everything we could in sight. After the extraordinary meal was finished, we both took time out to thank Arnold for making us into the fierce personas that he had so meticulously installed in us.

The Next Day, he dropped us off at the bus stop in his set-up blue Ford pickup truck. Before we hopped out of the car, he left us with one hundred dollars each, bullets for our brand-new 45mm pistols, and fair warning to proceed with caution about intervening into the lives of those intruders that stole our parents' precious lives from us.

"Promise me you don't go searching for them, they will probably try and meet up with you, unfortunately, in some type of street fight with guns ablaze. Now Rex, you're not a perfect target shot like your brother so proceed with caution. Trevor, you're no hand-to-hand combat like your sister."

"STAY SAFE...you hear me clearly?"

"Crystal clear," we both said in unison with evil grins on our faces. I silently contemplated several thoughts inside my mind. We were forced with the cumbersome burden of living in an unforgiving world with only each other to trust. I could only trust my brother? Still, on the upside of things, vengeance was ours overall. We were currently working on hurting a couple of sadistic murderers to bring back justice to our savagely butchered parents. We just didn't realize yet how the gun play, as nasty as it may be in the future, would turn out. Now we were both merely a shadow of a child...evolving into adulthood at such a young age, but desperately still clinging to every fabric of childhood we still had left. The great fabricated tapestry known as our life before these events all occurred...now gaining momentum into the unknown and unforgiving world of what was about to become unraveled out in the end.

CHAPTER THREE

Recovery from a Gun Shot Wound (Part 1)

Slowly regaining consciousness, I opened my eyes to reveal...

Absolutely nothing. Pitch black nothingness was the only item my lucid eyes were revealing to myself. Suddenly, panic began to set in when I hastily determined the possibility of complete blindness. Was this going to be the final stage of my very own vision...permanent blindness??? A heavy wetness seemed to be weighing down across my eyes. Quickly, I took my right hand to carefully inspect what was physically occurring to myself. After careful inspection, it was nothing more than...a heavy saturated cloth covering my eyes. Christ alive, I thought that I had just completely lost my eyesight. Thankfully, that was not the case. Currently, I was by myself in the hospital room. My jet-black hair was strewn across the provided hospital pillowcase. Eyes were as black as night, but decently hidden underneath a full set of thick black lashes. Hollowed high-end cheekbones and a small nose set off the rest of the features that made my face a bit plain and homely to the view of others. As a teenager, and a tomboy, I never saw my beauty... just my plain natural features.

There was a shimmering light filtering in through the blinds from the right corner of the room, everything else was completely shrouded in dimness and shadows. Adjusting to the lack of brightness in the room, my eyes took a second to regain a conscious estimation of exactly where I was located...a hospital bed where I was the patient instead of the visitor. Wincing in pain, I remembered the gunshot wound inflicted upon me by our own enemies. Peering down, underneath the hospital gown, I noticed the artistry of the various stitches under the clear dressing from the professional patch job that looked extremely well done.

I was re-living my previous past childhood. In my subconscious mind and the events that led up to this day…I drifted…I could remember by the second of every day till the event that almost ended my very own existence. Before I could lay my head back for some peace of mind, I heard a slight creak as the hospital room door slowly opened. Peeking through the slightly opened door, I saw Trevor looking in on me.

"Rex, are you doing all right?" asked Trevor with legitimate concern on his face…he proceeded into the room gingerly.

"Currently, I'm in a hospital bed recovering from gunshot wounds, Captain Obvious," I snapped. "How the hell do you think I'm just singing in the rain…just happy as can be"…I bolted in a lower pitched raspy alto voice.

"Maybe I will check back later." Trevor quickly replied and then retreated out of the room. The tranquil blessing of sleep returned mere minutes later.

That following day, I awoke to discover my brother Trevor sitting in a chair beside my hospital bed. His return to the hospital brought back to memory the vicious and mean spirited mannerisms I portrayed towards him previously. With that realization, I began to speak out,

"I really apologize for everything said yesterday, it was really out of line." Quickly apologizing gets rid of all the anger of being in the wrong, my father had previously said to me more than once.

"Oh Rex. That's understandable. Especially after everything we have recently gone through together. You pulled through great, you know, for being a pathetic scrawny girl and all," Trevor retorted.

"Man, bullshit!" *Where it rains, it pours*, I thought silently to myself.

"Excuse me, for a 'pathetic scrawny girl' I pulled through all right?"

"What the hell…get out of my room…NOW!!!" I bellowed in a much deeper and commanding voice than usual. Without hesitation, Trevor quickly shut the hospital door behind him.

Fucking men!

I screamed aggravated into the hospital pillow that I had been previously resting on before Trevor's pathetic outburst.

Unsure if it was the pain from the gunshot wound or my disdain for my brother at the time, I grew weary and quickly became listless and slept contentedly that afternoon.

——— Hours Later ———

I was in a deep sleep...until I heard a slightly raspy voice whisper something ominous within my ear that absolutely made my skin crawl. Gently, an unknown entity whispered in my ear:

"I thoroughly enjoyed putting a bullet straight through your mother's skull...."

I shot up from my hospital bed in terror to see who had quietly crept into my hospital room. Standing above me was a menacingly wretched looking woman that I knew instinctively was one of the two intruders that violated my sanctity of what once was our childhood home. From the corner of my left eye, I noticed something that completely un-nerved the already frayed nervous system I presently possessed. Two small squirts of some strange and unknown clear liquid quickly escaped from a syringe that the malicious intruder possessed in her hand.

"What the hell is that?" I quickly asked without seriously wanting any type of actual legitimate response. Fear of the unknown sort of wreaks havoc on the nervous system as well, so I figured I might as well deal with the horrific messes that are going to occur in mere moments.

"Actually the liquid is a pancuronium bromide it has one nasty side effect...paralysis of all functioning muscles in the body. Well, the universe won't end today, but your end is here, woman...." she said as she brought the syringe a bit closer to my exposed neck.

Glad there wasn't any venom attached to her words, I thought to myself silently. Unknowingly, while I was prompting her to talk as a sort of distraction, I had already pulled the emergency cord out of the wall. That went off as an alarm for the nurses to quickly run to my hospital room. Just before the intruder was about to inject the serum into my neck.

"Excuse me, what seems to be the problem?" one of the nurses asked in panic-stricken concern. "Oh my gosh!" she exclaimed....

"One of our nurses was found unconscious just around the corner... without her scrubs or identification badge," said the other nurse through clenched teeth.

Panic-stricken, the intruder with the syringe made a mad dash to the door knocking the nurses aside for a quick escape. One of the nurses sprinted over towards the intruder to try and put an immediate halt to her escape. Before the nurse could lay a hand on the intruder, the wretched woman who was trying to paralyze me opened the door... only to discover a police officer patiently waiting for someone to make the next hasty move out of pure ignorance. He just happened to be strolling on the same floor and knew something was wrong ahead of time, since another nurse previously called him out of another room.

"Where do you think you are going, miss?" questioned the officer with a slight sternness in his voice.

"I don't know where I'm going, officer, but I sure know where this syringe is going to end up," said the menacing woman and without a moment's hesitation viciously stabbed the syringe into his neck. The woman quickly darted down the hall.

Panic-stricken, he quickly grabbed the syringe from out of his neck without even clearly thinking. Suddenly, a huge spurt of blood shot out from his neck where the syringe had been viciously inserted by the intruder.

Without haste, he applied pressure to his neck with his right hand. Rushing over, one of the nurses from on the floor pushed him to safety behind the receptionist counter, then kneeled over the security officer's side for immediate assistance. While yelling to the other nurses for the crash cart.

"Hey, we need a surgeon STAT!" as she applied pressure to the ripped vessel.

Without hesitation, the other nurse ran in the opposite direction to call for emergency help and grabbed the emergency cart while I watched horrified by the entire scenario unfolding before my eyes.

CHAPTER FOUR

Recovery at Hospital (Part 2)

A few seconds later, a gurney with two workers and all sorts of staff arrived. "Type and cross for two units of blood. Wang's stat," barked a female doctor. The surgeon arrived and took his tool box, placing it on the cart. I was completely surrounded by staff. Someone grabbed me by the shoulders and aggressively escorted me out of the room. I was shaking uncontrollably over the gruesome scene I had previously witnessed.

"Thank you for the quick response, nurse Blanchard," said the nurse quickly with sincere gratitude in her voice.

"Not a problem," said the other nurse and then without haste, people were putting on their gloves, and with the help of a strong aid the security officer was hoisted onto the gurney and wheeled deeper into the room where the surgeon repaired the artery. Will he survive through the surgery? Many questions swam in my mind before I finally saw my brother Trevor hovering in front of the door frame.

"Rex...what just happened out there recently? Tell me what you know," Trevor quickly said before I began to sob uncontrollably.

"Just a few moments ago, I nearly died...again...when will this ever finally end? This is so stressful, I am going to flip out, Trevor you have no idea!!" I exclaimed in between tear stricken sobs of pure hatred. Hatred towards the very people that put me in this hospital room.... Hatred towards the very people that put my own loving parents into their own burial grave site!

I suddenly calmed down after several minutes of slowing the pacing of my breathing. I retold Trevor about the horrific recent events with the intruder, the nurses that arrived for help, and the injured security officer.

"Oh man! Glad you are safe, Rex. That's all that counts. Do you want me to check on the status of the police officer?"

"I will do that, by the way I am Thomas, the nurse supervisor. I will be right back." The nurse manager asked us if she could get us anything to drink. "No thanks, I'm fine," Trevor and I both said in unison. We saw the security guard wheeled out with several medical staff surrounding him.

"Well, with everything that has recently happened to you, I am here to find out if we can maintain your safety, without any further disturbances," replied Trevor as he took a chair to sit down beside mine. The nursing supervisor returned and said the officer will be taken to I.C.U. and he should recover.

"Thanks for everything, Trevor," I said, "I really mean it...." Trevor volunteered to stay with me for awhile....

Security called the nursing supervisor saying the intruder had been apprehended.

"She was the one that shot our mother point blank in the forehead," I remembered her now. I tilted my head and then clenched my teeth. Trevor was dead silent in the chair and developed a crimson face. The nursing supervisor, Trevor and I looked at each other. The nurse manager came out of the room.

"We are cleaning your room before we put you back in there. I am so sorry this happened." I leaned on the counter and put my head in my arms. I almost drifted off to sleep, I was so exhausted.

Escapism through sleep was not enough to flee that intruder's look on her face...the memory of her unforgettable countenance of pure hatred and capacity to kill without remorse was terrifying.

 ——— Hours Later ———

After I awoke, I quickly realized that I was left alone in the hospital room. Trevor was gone, but probably to get some information on the recently injured police officer.

Moments later, Trevor arrived with the up-to-date news about the injured police officer.

"Rex, currently that officer is out of critical status and is stable just down the hallway from you," said Trevor with less tightened tension from the jawline on his face than previously after the incident.

"Thanks for telling me the update, but I really wish they had apprehended the intruder." I quickly said as I turned my head away from him. The shame and guilt of not even being able to apprehend the intruder myself was just TOO much to handle.

"That's the news I was going to tell you, Rex...security at the exit gate caught the intruder!!" exclaimed Trevor in excitement.

"What? I thought she escaped," I gasped.

"No, Rex she is currently being interrogated at this very moment," said Trevor in high anticipation.

"Finally!!" we both screamed in unison.

After all these years, maybe motive could be in store for why the vicious murderers in cold blood dealt a death card to my own loving parents. He showed us pictures from the original crime scene. Suddenly, I began to re-live the previous tragic event in my own mind's eye. Tragically, I remembered my mother and father sitting at the dinner table with smiles on their faces.

Then, my mind fast forwarded to the tragic aftermath of the blood spattered patterns that adorned the table and floor of our safe haven... what we knew as home. He asked Trevor and I lots of questions and picked our brains for detailed past memories.

CHAPTER FIVE

Leaving the Hospital.... The Police Interrogation

Departure from the hospital was fairly routine, minus the stop Trevor and I made to visit the injured police officer.

"I can walk on my own, Trevor, I'm fine," I replied as he held onto my arm as I made my way into the police officer's hospital room.

"I know, Rex, but we can never take too many precautions. You just recently recovered from your surgery," whispered Trevor in my ear.

"Christ, whatever!" I said with stress and slight fatigue still residing within me.

As I slowly made my way over to the officer, I quickly noticed the gauze patch with a clear dressing over it that covered up the injury that was inflicted upon him. Slowly, he turned his head to witness who had entered his hospital room.

"Hello, Officer Blanchard, how are you feeling today?" asked Trevor with sincere concern. Suddenly, that name struck me as odd...*Blanchard...wasn't one of the nurses that helped the officer also named Blanchard?*

"Yes, I am related to nurse Blanchard, she's my sister," replied the officer as if he were secretly reading my very own thought processes.

Damn Psychic.

Anyways...

"Wow, she must have been really upset to see this happened to you," I replied.

"Yeah, I received a stern lecture about 'proper procedure' for when a hostile intruder is on the attack," he quickly rolled his eyes at the memory of that event.

"Well, we just wanted to visit with you for a second. We wanted to see how you were recovering," I replied.

"Thanks, I wish I could have really apprehended that intruder, but thank God their security on staff caught her on premises," said the officer with slight scorn reflected in his voice.

"Hey, at least that whacko is in custody now," Trevor quickly replied.

"Good, because I would have been kicking myself if she had escaped," replied the officer.

"Well, we have to go. So glad you will survive," I replied.

"God willing!!" replied the officer. Slowly, we made our exit out of his room, and later that same day, we made an exit out of the hospital.

Entering Their Precinct

Walking into the police department, I felt an extreme wave of nausea mixed with high levels of anxiety. I felt weak at the knees with my trembling hands but I quickly attempted to open the door leading into the police department.

"Wait, Rex," he grabbed me by the shoulders, "let me open that for you," Trevor said quickly as he moved in front of me to hold the door open.

"Glad you're handling this so well, after everything that we have been through together," I muttered under my breath.

Even growing up, I had to remember his mind-blowing optimism about almost everything. It outweighed my "practical" pessimism about most things in life.

As we made our way down the main hallway, we ended up at the front desk to ask where we would continue from there.

"Hello, how may I help you folks?" politely asked the front desk officer.

"There is a specific individual that the police have in custody now. The one that attacked your Officer Blanchard and then previously my sister," said Trevor quickly stammering over his words with seething emotion despite his attempt to keep a lid on it.

"Yes, that individual is currently being interrogated at this time, but you are both not allowed to make contact with that individual. Although, if you're willing to wait, you may take a seat in our visitor's room section. The officer in charge probably has some more questions for you. The duration of your wait time, unfortunately, is unknown," crisply said the attendant with crisp professionalism.

"Yes, we are willing to wait," we both said in unison.

Interrogation

Hand-cuffed and full of unrelenting coolness, the perpetrator was quickly guided into the pitch black interrogation room. After the officer flicked the lights on, you could at a second's glance sense the cold hatred emanating from the perpetrator. Without even having to be fully aware of what she was thinking. Did we truly want to know what this sick and twisted individual was thinking at that exact moment?

Prior to the interrogation, the officer sternly addressed her with the utmost professionalism.

"Before we begin anything, I would really like to make one thing clear. You are not escaping this room until I receive some real concrete answers from you."

"I want an attorney and I want one NOW...." Then the perpetrator quickly replied...

"Really? You think that you can just pry the words right out of my mouth? I have nothing to say, and you can't force me to say anything," said the female perpetrator with smooth contempt. The intruder spat the words out as if she were a rattlesnake full of venom while she sank her fangs in with each word that she vocalized. What the police officer soon would realize that people conceal the ugly things within, the intruder just lets them all out for the whole world to see!!!!!

"All right miss, I will give you a few minutes to cool down and collect your thoughts before we begin anything at all," said the officer with a matter-of-fact tone to his voice. A knock at the door came during the brief moment of silence. "I am the attorney to Miss Franchesca Russo, of the court."

Entering the interrogation room, the officer took up a chair and sat quietly down across from the female perpetrator. Quickly, the officer continued....

"So, are we ready to begin the interrogation proceedings?" asked the officer curtly.

Quietly, the intruder leaned in towards the officer with a look of hostility. "Why were you in the woman's hospital room?" The female perpetrator remained in complete and distant silence. "You don't have to answer," said her attorney, Michael Brenn. A mere twenty seconds later, she spit a huge wad of saliva straight into the officer's face. With a straight-faced blank stare, he wiped the saliva off his face....and then proceeded to eat it.

"Whoa dude, you're one sick idiot," replied the perpetrator.

"So, are we ready to begin?" asked the officer.

"I guess so, you're hard core man, and I thought I was top notch at that already," announced Russo with complete disgust.

"May I start with asking you what is your full name?" politely asked the officer. She remained silent...then she replied..."Franchesca Russo".

"No, wait, my real name is Rebekah Lynn Smith," she replied as she rolled her eyes at the officer.

"Is that your real name or did you just lie to me?" asked the officer incredulously.

"Of course that's not my real name, what do you think I am, a moron or something?" *Again with the eye rolling from this wretched woman*, thought the police officer silently to himself.

"Fine, enough with the smart comments from me. My real name is Franchesca Ann Russo."

"Russo...that name sounds familiar from somewhere, but I can't quite place where I have heard it previously," said the officer.

"Trust me, you would not know my family, they are actually quality," retorted Franchesca with no "surprising" hint of cynicism.

"So, that's why you're in interrogation now? Your family is in good graces with the law?" snottily retorted back the officer. Crimson faced, Franchesca quietly sat in her chair in calm, yet obvious, seething contempt towards the officer.

"Anyway, why were you trying to use that filthy syringe filled with the paralyzer on Rex?" asked the officer with sternness shown in his voice.

"You don't have to answer that…"said her lawyer.

"To finish some unfinished business," said Franchesca with cool contempt.

"Really? What unfinished business?" asked the officer, suddenly showing even more concern than previously.

"The unfinished business of killing Rex, I HATE THAT MORON!!! I would CURSE her very own name…. If God would allow me to…then sign me up for it!!!!" screamed Franchesca at the top of her lungs. Surprisingly, she spit quickly over her shoulder, superstitious enough to believe that it would ward that exact individual away from her momentarily. With pent up anger, she viciously slammed her head into the counter top of the red mahogany table. Repeatedly, again and again…until there was a small trickle of blood streaming down her face that was accompanied by a nasty bruise too. Laughing hysterically, she suddenly halted and whispered:

"You want to know my little secret, officer? My brother and I kill… just for the DAMN fun…the thrill of the hunt…killing…AIN'T NOTHING BETTER!!"

"STOP!" Yelled her lawyer, "again, you do not have to answer. I advise you not to answer at all!" said the lawyer abruptly. Franchesca had insanity written on her face. "I object! Franchesca!" Her lawyer interjected, "this interview is OVER! We wish that Miss Russo needs to be taken back to her cell!"

Stubbornly, the officer rolled his eyes and then walked across to take Franchesca back into her cell.

"You say nothing until your trial…do you understand me?" pleaded the lawyer with panicked concern emanating from his voice.

"Crystal clear," said Franchesca solemnly as the officer proceeded to take her back to her cell.

Living in the "metal hell" known previously as her prison cell, Franchesca briefly thought about ending her own life. Suddenly, a brief glimpse into the future put Franchesca on the stand at trial. The real facts about why their parents had to be killed might be…amusing to see the kids' reactions, to say the least, Franchesca sadistically smiled at the mere thought of that future event.

"Hope those kids are ready for what I'm about to say at trial," Franchesca said quietly to herself before turning in to get some much needed sleep for the night.

Later, the officer entered the visitor's room where Rex and Trevor were waiting patiently.

"Thanks for waiting, may I tell you some of the results that were revealed to me?" asked the officer.

"Yes," Rex and Trevor said in unison.

"Well, I discovered that Franchesca led us towards a confession, but, unfortunately, nothing can be confirmed until the trial begins and the judge has made his final verdict," said the officer with crisp professionalism.

"So…she basically confessed to everything so let's just end it with her already…out of existence from us," Trevor said with enthusiasm.

"Sorry folks, we need to conduct a trial first, but if you would like to testify…"

"On our parents' behalf, you better believe we will be present at trial," Rex said adamantly.

"I figured that much," but he quickly handed Rex his business card, "I will be talking to you some time next week with further details pertaining to the future trial," said the officer with his crisp talking professionalism once again.

"So, we're done here until next week?" asked Trevor.

"Basically," said the officer and then immediately left the room to go straight back to his office.

"All right, let's get out of here Trevor," I quickly said, "waste of our time, and all we here is 'Basically' after they know that stupid—"

"Rex! End it!" yelled Trevor, "I don't want you causing a scene here, we're not sinking down to their level," said Trevor adamantly.

"Whatever," I replied and then quickly we both exited the police department.

CHAPTER SIX

Mysterious Calls

Sitting at home, I received a mysterious call from an unknown source.

"Why the hell is my sister locked in a cell downtown at the police department?!"

"Do you even realize why your parents died?"

"What motivated us to complete that..." Dial tone was all I heard then a distinct clicking noise as the caller on the receiving end abruptly hung up the phone.

"What the hell?!" I exclaimed in light of the strange events that recently occurred. I was suddenly dumb-founded by the recent event. I leaned back in my seat. For a moment, I forgot to breathe so I took a deep breath. Finally, after a few moments of silence, I heard a knock on the door.

Trevor cocked his head then stood up from his chair and quickly made his way over to the door. Trevor slowly crept to the door and opened it. On the ground, a step away from his right foot, was something truly horrific. Shining with a slimy film of translucent membrane was one fully open pair...of eyes.

"AAHH!" screamed Trevor at the top of his lungs.

"Trevor, what's wrong?!" I ran over to investigate and I discovered the pair of eyes on our doorstep, I could only react with one pure emotion: FEAR.

"Call 911!" I commanded to Trevor and he complied. He dialed quickly with trembling hands and was transferred to the Rochester Police who commanded us not to touch anything and help was on the way.

"Sure thing! I will make sure no one touches this, it's evidence now," said Trevor. Moments later, he and I were being questioned by the police, I could only think of one question for them:

"Why?!" "Are those human eyes?" "Why would someone consider doing that?" "Are they fucking weird or what?" I heard in reply the very generic phrase: "We're working on that, ma'am."

"Our department will be in touch. Sorry about the incident, there are a bunch of psychos out there and considering other recent events; we will do our best to find out who instigated this incident."

Five minutes later, the police were gone. Mysteriously, a second phone call began to ring from inside the house.

"No rest for the wicked," I said. We both ran in to see who the caller was this time.

"I will pickup the phone now," commanded Trevor; I decided to sit down in a chair. He picked up the receiver and heard a menacing tone on the other end of the line:

"I see you with my OWN pair of eyes…even right as we're speaking now." -click- The caller quickly ended the call on that ominous note.

"What the hell?!" shouted Trevor. I felt drained, being recently released from the hospital.

"I know! That's what I said the first time! Now you know how I feel…" I said with sweet relief that I wasn't the only person in the house being played.

"You need to go to bed. You are pale, it looks as if your very own life force has been slowly drained out of your entire face!" said a very concerned Trevor.

"Fine, I am going to sleep," I finally said.

The Next Day, we were visited again by the Rochester police. The same generic responses and questions were asked in brisk Boston brogue accents. After feeling as if no one really cared; they quickly recommended at the time to have security in a patrol car around the corner.

One officer took a call from the police department, "Ok sergeant…All right. I will look into it, bye." He resumed questioning us without a beat.

"After investigating, we have concluded that the eyes found at your door step were that of a crime probably an Australian shepherd breed.

Also, pertaining to Franchesca, her hearing will be held on May 1st, 2012 at 10:30 a.m. sharp. Please attend and wear business casual to the hearing. Sorry about the wait but this is record timing for us. Best regards, from our police department. Hopefully, this female perp gets put behind bars for a long time." After a moment of silence I said, "Hey, doesn't our neighbor have an Aussie dog?"

"Yeah," said Trevor with a sickening look on his face.

"An Australian shepherd," Trevor looked at me and our eyes met.

The unknown was already known in just one moment of silence.

CHAPTER SEVEN

An Unfortunate Dead Shepherd

"I wonder if the neighbor's dog is missing," I said while pouring a bowl of cereal.

"Maybe WE should check," said Trevor. "I want this crazy mess solved...pronto!!!" Said Trevor as he walked towards the door.

"Christ, I hope it's not their dog...." I said as quickly as Trevor shut the door behind us.

Moments later, we both gave a slight knock on our neighbors door. We stood there patiently waiting after knocking, a minute or two. We heard footsteps. Finally, the neighbor opened the door after shouting, "Who is it?!"

"It's your neighbors Trevor and Rex," we shouted in unison.

"What seems to be the problem?" asked our neighbor with legitimate concern.

"Is it any information on our missing dog?"

"We were going to send out flyers...." Suddenly, I cut to the chase and quickly blurted out:

"He's dead...your dog was savagely murdered by a sadistic idiot!" I realized the words flew out of my mouth, before the foot insert I should have blatantly done previous to saying anything at all.

"What!" exclaimed the neighbor incredulously. Before she could say anything else, the neighbor's daughter ran up to her mother and wrapped her small arms around her left leg. Pointing with her small left index finger she shouted, "There's a crazy person in the woods!" Then she quickly uttered an uncontrollably terrifying scream that still rings through my very own ears to this exact day. Swiftly, we all turned our heads in unison to the exact location the child was pointing towards in the woods. Through the trees, you could make out the shape of a man carrying something a bit odd in his left hand. It was fluffy, no, furry with ears, a nose, a blood splattered mouth and that horrid looking....

It had two gaping holes where the eyes should have been located. The man in the woods was holding up the dead dog's head of the beloved Australian shepherd the family had grown to adore and love. Now, it was nothing more than decaying flesh, rotted out tongue, and a few maggots writhing and squirming in and out of its non-existent eye sockets.

Screaming in unison, everyone continued to stare at the horrific sight of this heinous crime.

Flashing lights suddenly appeared off in the near distance. Swerving into the driveway, the officer put the patrol car in park and quickly got out of the vehicle.

"Just patrolling the area at just the right time...heard some screaming off in the distance and I thought about stopping in for a second. What seems to be the problem? What's going on?" The officer looked around quickly and then noticed some movement in the woods...like someone running away from us??

"Quick, after that man, officer, he murdered their dog!" exclaimed Trevor. "Had his damn decapitated head in his ugly wretched left hand! Come on, let's go!" I bellowed out the words before anyone else could get a word in edgewise. Swiftly, the officer made a mad dash towards the movement in the woods. Upon arrival, there was a moment of silence that seemed to take an eternity. Suddenly, after the deadly silence, came something a bit more lively. Off in the distance you could hear the remote sound of a gun being cocked, brush being broken and two fired-off gun barrel shots being exchanged in the utter chaos of it all. Moving towards the two gun barrel shots, we found a quite disturbing scene. The officer had a naked man pinned down on the ground while he quickly placed handcuffs on him before he could cut loose and escape. To the left of the man were the remains of what seemed to be a gutted out animal...canine breed...an Australian shepherd.

"Oh Christ…Marie…don't…look in front of you!"…she quickly clamped her right hand over her small innocent child's eyes to avoid the gruesome sight. Suddenly, when the hand-cuffed man slowly lifted his head up from the ground, everyone discovered something revolting. In the left side corner of his mouth looked like splattered blood…some entrails remnants…did he seriously just recently eat a portion of that dog? Like some type of satanic ritual? Or a self-proclaimed sacrifice to some unknown deity! Insanity!

"I cannot believe what you just did!" screamed our neighbor in unrelenting terrified rage. Suddenly, she continued on… "Why did you do that? You're a complete stranger! Why? What did we ever do to you?" Her anger was quickly rising with each breath she was taking.

Quickly, the hand-cuffed man looked her dead in the eye and replied: "Existing…you with your perfect little bubble of a world… someone had to just stop by and burst it." To further his cause, he sadistically smiled at her.

The blood in her veins ran ice cold in front of the sadistic man that viciously killed their most beloved precious puppy.

Before anything else could escalate, the officer quickly escorted the naked man to the back of the patrol car, commanding him to straighten up and later proceeded to quickly drive off. In the conundrum that started around us Trevor and I looked at each other again. People were asking what happened. We shrugged our shoulders simultaneously. No one knew the true intentions of a mad man. Questioning and interrogation of that man, we would soon find out, would be a quite interesting turn of events.

CHAPTER EIGHT

Interrogation of a Mad Man

"The only way we're going to figure this out is after that man's interrogation is over!" said Trevor to me the next day as I sat sulking in my chair.

"Wow, I still have that picture in my mind of those canine eyes on our door step.... Then that insane look on the man's face wasn't making anything better," I said as I put my hands around my head to calm myself.

Trevor and I were called in to testify at the station. We were patiently waiting for the end of the interrogation when an officer had the now "clothed" man sitting across from him in the interrogation room. We stood behind the one way window.

"Is this the man you saw last night with a dog's head?"

"Absolutely," I said and Trevor nodded in reassurance.

"What do you have to say for yourself?" said the officer.

"Do you have any idea the significant damage mentally you have caused towards these people?" A moment of silence passed over the two of them. Suddenly, the perpetrator spoke:

"Listen, officer, I am the one that chose my own path in life, no matter how black or macabre that may seem to you. Do you realize it's part of a ritual?" he half smiled sadistically.

"What the hell?" The officer blurted out before the perpetrator could even get a word in edgewise.

"Well," the perpetrator continued on, "it's part of a ritual practiced to warn people of certain upcoming events."

"Sure...like what?" asked the officer.

"Death," coolly replied the perpetrator.

"So, you're telling me that the dead and bloated carcass of an innocent dog was part of one of your rituals?" asked the officer with his head cocked back in disbelief.

"Yes," replied the perpetrator matter-of-factly.

"Help me understand what exactly you're talking about when you say...RITUAL...let's get down to business here Mr....what is your name again?" asked the officer quickly.

"Ethan...Russo," replied the perpetrator as he narrowed his eyes at the police officer.

"Ethan Russo...sounds like a particular last name I have heard in the past few days," said the officer.

"Well, I am sure that you have, seeing as that my sister is someone you have already incarcerated...FRANCHESCA RUSSO."

Behind the viewing windowpane, Trevor and I gasped in unison.

"Yeah, Ethan's sister in crime is Franchesca...figures." I said underneath my breath.

"We did your stupid parents in!" yelled Ethan at our window as he made a slicing motion across his throat as if he were imagining completing that task towards our innocent parents.

"Settle down!" commanded the interviewer. Another knock at the door dominated the room for the next round of successful noises to bother the beating heart that was drumming in my chest simultaneously. Ethan's attorney stormed in at that exact moment.

"This interview is OVER!"

After the interrogation we headed over to the car to make a clean get away from all the previous chaos.

"It's always something, now we know the faces of who committed those heinous crimes toward our parents," I said through strewn out bitter tears of resentment. Only after the interrogation would I actually break down to cry...but not in front of those two sadistic people...NEVER.

"How do you know that for sure, Rex?" asked Trevor with slight apprehension.

"Well, Trevor, the two are brother and sister. We already have a confession about it from Franchesca. One man and one woman that infiltrated our home. They even fit the body type and his confession seals the deal on that part. Those two are..."

"Dead," Trevor finished the end of my sentence, perfectly indicating what they truly deserved…death.

"Want to wait for the court to decide or take matters into our own hands?!" I asked Trevor.

"Rex…" said Trevor cautiously.

"Fine," I said rolling my eyes… "patience is a virtue."

CHAPTER NINE

Pre-Trial Jitters

As a plaque adorned behind the judge Lady Justice had her self-proclaimed head held up to the heavens for fair legal justice. She would weigh her symbolic scales upon the case to finalize her overall justice.

In this exact room, Lady Justice would have her final say as to the verdict on what occurred during the massacre of our parents. It was a pre-trial hearing today.

We made our way into the court room. My heart began to race as I came to the dreadful realization of the perpetrators who intruded violently into our lives. They would recount what had happened…from the exact side of their horrific story.

Quickly looking over at my brother Trevor, I noticed he was equally as nervous. Perspiration on his brow matched with a look of deep sorrow was accompanied by something else…contempt. For the intruders, for the legal system, for the injustice of it all.

Hell had no wrath like a human being scorned, I silently thought to myself. Quietly, we took our seat off in the corner of the room beside an officer.

Infinite amounts of time stood at a standstill as we anxiously awaited what would happen next. Finally, Michael Brenn, Franchesca Russo's lawyer, walking in with the utmost professionalism, came into the courtroom. "Why the hell am I here?" I asked myself. "Everyone already knows that he is defending pure evil.. why bother with them?" Quietly, he then proceeded to take his seat at one side of the remaining table and chair. His briefcase was the only sole friend without a purpose he had…or so we thought at that exact time.

After a few moments of silence, the county prosecutor showed up dressed in a crisply tailored pinned stripped black business suit, an expensive one. Quickly, he took his seat on the other side of the room. His name was Brandon Smith, I believe, known for his hard as brass tacks prosecutorial skills. Top notch, top of the line prosecuting attorney…paid for by county taxes.

"I hope he eventually really makes those two sorry excuses of garbage pay for what they did to our parents," I quietly leaned into Trevor. "Agreed" was the only quick response my brother had at that exact time. Next came the worst part of it all. Better yet, utmost miscreant filth of society decided to show up into the courtroom.

Franchesca looked like hell in a hand basket in an orange jumpsuit. Her dark eyes were sunken in from lack of sleep. Puffy bags underneath her eyes were another indicator that sleep was not acquired the previous night. Her auburn brown hair was neatly pinned back in a ponytail. Still, that face…it was as if a witch from a horror film and a troll mated…to give birth to that wretched woman. She walked slowly, in chains, as if there were literally a heavy burden weighing down on her shoulders. Hunched over, she quietly made her way over to her seat and sat in the chair.

Slowly, she swiveled her head to look me dead in the face. Suddenly, a sadistic smile began to play on Franchesca's lips. She mouthed the word "Hello" and tried to innocently wave at me.

"That little…" I began to say something, but was silenced by my brother's reassuring words:

"It's not our fault Rex, it's theirs and Lady Justice will have the final say today," said Trevor as he patted my hand to ease my mind.

I rolled my eyes impatiently at his response and quickly pulled my hand away to quietly fold my arms in front of me in a defensive posture.

"They deserve to die!" I quietly muttered my determined conviction towards my brother. The other intruder arrived in the courtroom. Like an eyesore found in the seventh circle of hell, his look was not any better than Franchesca's at all. Puffy bags underneath his dark eyes that were blood shot red from lack of sleep. His eyes gave him a haggard bum-like look. Surprisingly, his hair also was immaculate and groomed well to perfection. The rest of him…not so perfect. His orange jump suit was rumpled.

"I bet they have seen better days than today," Trevor whispered beside me.

"Their days are numbered, it is just a matter of time for them now. They just did not realize until this exact moment." I whispered back through clenched teeth. Quietly, he staggered his way over to a chair by Franchesca and sat down. Their lawyer, Michael Brenn, was sitting in the middle of the two of them. A team of suits were now suddenly noticed seated behind their desk quietly conferring. A moment of silence passed within the courtroom. "All rise," the officer of the court bellowed. The judge made his way into the courtroom. Everyone stood up for a moment before the judge said, "You may be seated." Everyone complied and went back to their original seating.

"All right, I would like to hear the defendants' case statement and then the prosecuting attorney's," the judge stated sternly.

Michael Brenn, the defendant's lawyer, calmly stood up before the judge and said:

"Your honor, I believe that these two people are actually not guilty due to an insanity plea...."

"Bull **it," my eyes narrowed and I started to say something really nasty, but held myself back for that moment. Judge Harvard's mallet came down once.

"Furthermore," he continued on, "I believe that they both have evidence of some type of delusional state of mind where their perceived ideas of actual reality are a bit...misguided."

Their lawyer, with steadfast determination, handed out a two-page memorandum to the judge. "This is a specified statement from a mental health facility that clearly states how they both are not of any practical sound mind or reasonable judgment at all."

"Furthermore, it ends with a recommendation about several reasons why both should be admitted as patients of a very specified mental health facility."

"Blah, Blah, Blah," I whispered to Trevor while he had a look of stern disapproval on his face.

Suddenly, the lawyer took his seat and decided to leave the rest in the professional hands of the judge.

The prosecutor then rose up and stood in front of the judge to candidly tell his case statement.

"Today, the jury is not present at this time but I want the truth to be known by everyone that those two (he quickly pointed at the defendants) are just two calculated, cold blooded killers. Instead of an insanity plea, your honor, I can prove they are guilty on all counts. Furthermore, I can prove these two innocent kids (now adults) that had their parents brutally murdered from the perpetrators. Their entire intent was completely pre-meditated. Both were trespassing on private property intending to…KILL. That they later tortured and terrorized an innocent animal to scare these young people recently and I intend to prove they are a part of a very menacing cult. This cult requires killing as a sacrifice to their God. Their god is called Demuke.

"I intend to prove not only that they were into pre-meditated murder, a heinous torturer of an innocent animal has killed before. The word 'insanity,' your Honor, to cover up their true intent is a cult that kills its own members who want to escape from the membership to personal freedom." Both opposing lawyers handed over the judge their carefully calculated witness lists and exhibit lists too.

"All rise," bellowed an officer.

While this was all occurring, the jury party arrived and was instructed to all meet together and agree upon the instructions given to everyone. The judge sternly explained the important topic of no talking about the case with anyone. He made it clear they would be replaced if they discussed the case with anyone. After the pre-trial hearing, which lasted two hours, Trevor and I walked out feeling emotionally drained. The remembrance of past events and loved ones gone forever tends to put a damper on just about everything imaginable.

"Let's go home, Rex," said Trevor as he held the car door open for me.

"Yeah, I feel drained out, Trevor, let's go," I said as I got into the car.

Moments later, we drove off with a slight reassurance that this, at the beginning of the end, might be one COLD case eventually solved.

CHAPTER TEN

A Lesson Learned

On the day of the trial, I felt my stomach tied up in several knots. As time waned on, I began to feel sicker. I was dreading the process of the upcoming hearing, I sat down and turned on the television set to get my mind off of everything. Shaken by recent events, all I could remember in my mind's eye was the twisted head of Franchesca staring me dead in the eye...then the gruesome twisted smile that made me sick to my stomach. Reeling from the memory, I felt as if a spider was trying to cast a web of lies and deceit around everything and anything I truly cared about in this world...my parents, memories of them, and my very own vulnerable sanity.

Later, Trevor and I left to drive over to the courthouse, I felt as if hundreds of eyes were focused on both of us. The sick feeling seemed to intensify, until I finally closed my eyes for a moment to regain my composure.

"How are you feeling, Rex?" asked Trevor with legitimate concern.

"Fine, just calming myself before this trial proceeds," I quickly said, not realizing that Trevor was paying close attention to my demeanor.

"I know those two psycho killers are finally going to get what's coming to them by the legal justice system," said Trevor with a surprising amount of venom emanating from his voice. "Justice is a slow and unwinding road," he added.

"I agree" was all that I said before we were escorted quietly into the courtroom.

"These are the ties that bind...Family...Honor...and Justice...for our brutally murdered parents. Let's go in that courtroom today knowing that justice will be served." He fiercely hugged me for further reassurance. After that being said by Trevor, we finally were escorted into the courtroom.

Crushing waves of nausea hit me when I saw that Franchesca and her brother were sitting down beside their lawyer. Quickly, I looked away from both as my mind reeled with previous events.

"I can't wait until all of this chaos is over, I need some well-deserved rest," said Trevor. His puffy bagged eyes appeared to be almost swollen shut.

"Agreed" was my quick response. I looked down.

I could sense a black macabre of evil essence that could be almost visibly seen but truly felt in the aura of the brother and sister. You could almost smell the sulfur from where they were originally created... possibly in the ninth circle of hell.

Moments later, the judge calmly approached the bench.

"All rise, your honorable Judge Haggard presiding." Obviously, everyone in the courtroom stood up. Moments passed, then an officer announced, "You may be seated," and we all sat as directed.

Moments of silence passed, then the defense attorney calmly approached the bench to share his official statement with the jury.

He began by stating, "Obviously, I am here to protect the best interests of the two (he quickly pointed towards them) people I am currently defending. In my honest and professional opinion, I believe that it is in the best interest of the people for both defendants to seek the utmost professional mental health care in an established professional setting.

"Furthermore, I am willing to fight for an insanity plea due to the graphic nature of abuse that they experienced while being members of a cult. Now, not as a means of a get out of free jail card, but as the right method to properly seek the utmost care for these individuals to reduce another set-back or 'episode' if you will...please forgive me; these terms are not at all technical. Seeing as that I am a defense lawyer, instead of a mental health facilitator, I would give legitimate reasons as to why they need this specified help from a professional mental health attendant."

Quietly, he paused for a moment and for dramatic emphasis, folded his hands behind his head.

"The mind is a very fragile entity. Most brain development is retained between ages of newborns to the age of five. Yet, the human mind is still not fully developed until age twenty-five. Still, due to the cult they were in, any manipulation or 'brain-washing' of the mind during this time could leave a very distorted or even disturbing sense of distinguishing right from wrong."

Calmly, he approached the jury and responded, "If your daughter or son had a mental disorder...wouldn't you want the utmost care provided?" asked the attorney staring down one member of the jury.

"Enough! Last statement ignored, it leads to coercion and that is not allowed in my courtroom, sir," the judge bellowed out in a deep raspy voice.

"Very well, sir, as you wish," said the defense attorney. Next, through pictures, he began showing around five different proofs of evidence to finalize his theory on an insanity plea. First, blown up to a bigger than life picture frame size, the picture depicted what seemed to be some type of ritual. No, actually it was some type of cannibalism. I couldn't tell what was worse, the dead animal cadaver in the center of the table, or the fact that two small children were literally devouring the innards of the animal...with sadistic smiles on their faces. Waves of horror could be witnessed on many of the faces in the jury. To their horror, the defense attorney continued on with the statement:

"Since the two children in the picture may come as a shock for you all to know...they are Franchesca and her brother during a very celebratory 'festival' that typically occurs around our Christian Christmas time. Wait...before I say anything further..." The defense attorney slowly began to point out both of their faces, "If that is any resemblance of 'normal' behavior from children...I rather find this particular picture to be of a very graphic and most disturbing nature."

The entire jury completely gasped in unison.

"What are the secrets behind the smiles of those children?" asked the defense attorney.

"The real secret to uncover is whether those pictures are Franchesca and her brother." I quietly murmured to myself.

"When my clients take the stand, that all will be revealed in due time," said the attorney coolly.

A few moments passed, then the second picture was revealed. This specific picture revealed the family's best version of what they considered true normalcy...their entire family was dressed entirely in white, and were looking very pristine and professional. Until we all noticed what was underneath their feet...blood soaked underneath their pale bare feet.

"Honestly, in this picture, that is not actual blood at all, but rather, their depiction of how people may seem truly pure at first...but quite the opposite when they reveal their 'true' selves. Sadly," he continued on, "due to the graphic nature of the third picture, the judge will not allow it as any type of evidence in the courtroom."

He took a sweeping glance at the entire jury and then quietly sat down at his small bench area. Next, the defense quietly brought up Franchesca's brother towards the stand to sit down. No matter how hard I tried, I still revealed bitter tears of resentment streaming down my face. Feeling like a coward, I slowly covered my face for a moment to regain my composure.

"It's all right, Rex," said Trevor reassuringly as I felt his hand clamp down on my right shoulder, for moral support during the current situation.

"These are the ties that bind. Family, honor, and justice...for our brutally murdered parents...let's stay in this courtroom today knowing that justice will be served."

Bright, just break down right in front of the sadistic idiot, I thought silently to myself. After sworn in, the defense attorney began again, "Now, the defense brings Franchesca's brother to the stand." A hushed moment of silence fell over the entire courtroom.

Suddenly, the defense attorney began by asking, "Could you please re-tell your version of the exact night that you made contact with Rex and Trevor's parents?" he asked as he slowly approached Franchesca's brother. A moment of silence passed. Quickly, Franchesca's brother cleared his throat before he began to re-count the exact event.

"Well, it all began when their parents decided that they did not want to be members of our congregation anymore." He said with beads of perspiration slowly gaining momentum on his forehead.

"What do you mean by anymore?" asked his defense attorney.

"They used to be members, well actually, recruits we wanted to turn into members of our congregation. "

"What made their parents suddenly change their mind?" asked the defense attorney.

Shifting nervously back and forth in his seat, Franchesca's brother finally revealed the actual cold hard truth.

"Human sacrifice upon an immediate entrance into the congregation. They were not too keen on the idea, which is only something we have to initiate to get to the actual 'becoming' membership level." Said her brother so coolly you would have thought that he was simply instructing a child on how to screw in a light bulb into a socket.

"To clarify, sir, what do you specifically mean when you say the exact word 'becoming'?" asked the defense attorney, looking a bit confused at his defendant for the moment.

"The 'becoming' process is really the final step in gaining access to full membership into our congregation."

"After making a human sacrifice (as long as it is not a child nor an elder) is made towards our God Demuke—"

"Sorry, I did not mean to interrupt, but just for clarification…what exactly does your god Demuke look like if you were to actually witness him?" asked the defense attorney.

"Demuke looks like a cross-breed between a human and a demon. The overall look is a male human, yet his hair is actually ignited in orange and red combustible flames. The flames are always slowly dancing around the frame of his ashen face. A strong jaw-line with pitch black eyes sets off the omen of the unknown…our dark lord known as Demuke." This was all said by Franchesca's brother in such a cryptic tone of voice, that the entire courtroom was literally silent for a straight five-minute window of time.

Trevor leaned in to whisper, "I understand you're both insane, but you are not getting away with murdering our parents. I just don't care for their overall indecent lies."

"Agreed" was all that I could barely say while my eyes were completely glued on the defendant at that exact moment in time.

"Rantings of a sane individual? I am afraid not…" began the defense attorney.

"Sorry," Franchesca's brother leaned in to the judge and whispered, "may I finish my explanation about the membership process into our congregation?"

"Yes, you may proceed, sir" was the only quick response given by the judge.

"As I was previously explaining…so begins the stage to full on membership due to the sacrifice is seen to Demuke as the ultimate sign of enlightenment to reach a heightened state of mind." He coolly said without any hesitation whatsoever.

"Heightened state of mind? Can you please clarify that statement for the jury?" asked the skeptical attorney.

"We believe that people that our in extreme amounts of pain should be put out of their misery. Such examples are terminally diagnosed cancer patients, anyone with malignant tumors, or those with unknown yet incurable diseases.

"We give them their 'final sacred rites' if you will, and then end their suffering on this earth."

"Wait, so you believe this to be a sane, logical, and practical religion?" asked the attorney.

"Yes," said her brother without even the slightest indication of remorse.

"Without any further discussion, I would like to take him off the stand and bring in Franchesca for questioning." Crisply said the attorney with the utmost professionalism.

"Very well then," said the judge quickly, "you may proceed."

"Christ, you have got to be kidding me. The three-ring narcissistic freak side show is about to make her grand entrance," I whispered towards Trevor as I simultaneously rolled my eyes at the mere thought. Her on the testifying stand in all of her macabre, self-serving indignation, and me just a silent observer with nothing to do but watch her three-ring circus act make her live debut performance…yet would the jury buy into an insanity plea? Or figure out the true cruel and inhumane creature that is possessed within her being?

Silently pleading to God, I closed my eyes and swore I would be more faithful if only he granted me this one wish…her frying carcass in an electric chair. Upon opening my eyes…wish truly not granted at all.

"Christ alive!" I almost screamed out loud in the courtroom. Franchesca was already on the testifying chair, and she was staring at me. The staring was quite unsettling. A mixture of evil dementia and sadistic glee overtook her demeanor as she quickly said:

"I'm ready to talk about everything, I have nothing to hide at all."

A hushed moment of silence fell over the courtroom and then she furthered her diabolical cause by saying, "You know the true ideology of messiahs? They're just a very misguided and false overall prophet."

She said all this while staring at me in a sick mannerism that made my skin crawl.

Silently I thought to myself...never heard of the term "resurrection" Franchesca?

"Franchesca, I would like to directly order you to make eye contact with your attorney ONLY at this present time. Thank you," said the judge without hesitation. The mere look that she gave me recently put chills up and down my skin. Glad that the judge made his quick commentating, I closed my eyes and tried for a moment to regain my composure.

"Are you sure you can handle all of this?" asked my brother with concern shown within his voice.

"Yeah, I can handle it. I just have to remain calm and not make anymore direct eye contact with Franchesca.... It's very unsettling, Trevor."

"They are both EXTREMELY dedicated to being a complete sadistic bitch towards both of us...that judge quickly will come unglued on them." Said Trevor with one eyebrow raised in an unforgiving thought that not even I could deduce as his only sibling.

Suddenly, the defense attorney began to communicate again with Franchesca about further explanation specifically about her religion.

"Could you please explain to the courtroom a traditional ritual that would occur at your congregation? Just to clarify for everyone in the room..." he said while making a sweeping motion across the room specifically towards the jury. The smirk on his face was a bit TOO self-righteous, so I knew something big was going to happen that would truly help out the defense...yuck!

Franchesca began, "The first traditional ritual we conduct starts with cutting a baby goat by the throat and then letting it bleed out into a medium-size black bowl.

"Then we smear the baby goat's blood on our throat as remembrance that we shall 'speak no evil' unless under attack by a sworn enemy, usually seen as an unbeliever. After that, everyone in the congregation yells their praises at the same time for our dark lord Demuke."

Honestly, after her last sentence, I thought she might just happen to have a resemblance of joy that sickened me to the very core of my own vulnerable soul...unless she ended up stealing it by the end of the trial.

The defense attorney verbally leaped in after she made that statement:

"So, members of the jury, do you believe these statements to be those of a sane and rational individual? Did their ritual remotely sound like anything that had sanity intact with it? Honestly, I am afraid not..." Then without further hesitation, he quickly made his way back to his seat.

Finally, our hero of the hour, the prosecution went up to quickly question Franchesca after that vicious display of overall bull shit, just to get away with murder. Hell, on a technicality...isn't that the main basis for most insanity pleas in a courtroom? Anyways...

Trevor and I could barely contain our excitement as he began to question the defendant:

"So, you seem like a shrewd business woman, Franchesca. Is your 'fake' religion just another complicated scam to legally take hard earned money away from decent people?" he asked as he candidly looked at the jury.

"Excuse me? What are you implying?" asked Franchesca with a deep crimson face filled with a mixture of rage and embarrassment. The mere comment alone sent her into a fit of rage. She carried on with further indignation:

"How dare you imply such a thing! I will have you know that my allegiance is with Demuke, and there is nothing you can do to stop me. Your CHRISTIAN faith and your CHRISTIAN god are DEAD, long live Demuke!!!!!" she insanely screamed (Trevor and I believe to further her insanity plea) to the point where everyone was covering their ears for possible sound barrier protection. The judge quickly bellowed out:

"I refuse to have another occurrence of a disruption in my courtroom. I want order in my courtroom. Immediately!" sternly said the judge while hammering down his gavel into his fairly ethical bench. A moment of silence fell over the entire courtroom. A few minutes later, the prosecuting attorney carried on with the statement:

"Isn't it extremely difficult to be that hostile and angry when you take advantage of your congregation's money?" calmly asked the attorney.

"Give an example, prove that I am wrong," said Franchesca with a glance of hatred so dominant, it could have made even the man of steel fly in the other direction.

"Well, is it true that you give free room and board for up to six months if only your congregation members pay up $1,000 upon their induction for full-membership into the congregation?" asked the attorney as he leaned in so close to Franchesca's face, they could have been almost touching the ends of each other's noses.

Taken back a bit, Franchesca carried on with a strange statement.

"Well, only to those who believe in Demuke the most faithful believers that we acquire into our congregation. It is just one intricate part in pledging their alliance," said Franchesca with grim determination.

"Well, with your 'true believers' as you call it, why do you make them run all of your errands and complete all of your housework chores...like some type of indentured servant through membership?" asked the prosecuting attorney with a quizzical look on his face.

"For the free room and board...that's what they owe us," plainly said Franchesca.

"Even with the initial $1,000 that you make your willing congregation members pay out every two to three months just to simply stay there? By the way," the attorney continued on, "how many people exactly live there?"

"Between ten and fifteen people, it really varies," said Franchesca nervously.

"Varies...that sounds interesting," said the attorney and walked back towards his bench momentarily to pick up some piece of evidence.

"Do you recognize these three official documents?" asked the attorney. Suddenly, he slammed the pieces of paper down on the testifying bench in front of Franchesca.

"Three eviction notices from three members of your truly dedicated congregation. They had to sell their homes to afford your payments... out of what? Greed? Some mere delusional sense of dedication to a false god? Wow, you really had that insanity plea rolling for you, until you fucked it up. You're a con artist instead, and a damn good one at that. You believe that you can get away with the brutal murder of (he quickly pointed to Trevor and myself) their parents? Insane, no, let's try for a manipulative con artist instead that puts a false god in front of people, tells them to worship that false god, and then you both hold out your willing hands for some monetary compensation." He said while glaring at her the entire time with a look of pure contempt on his face.

"Also," he added, "is it true that you force your congregation members to pay some additional fee to be able to participate in that congregation? Please, tell me the exact amount, Franchesca." The attorney had such a look of pure hatred towards Franchesca, I almost thought that he would have dealt out some cold justice towards her in the form of a literal fighting arena match.

"$1,000 once they pass initiation and that guarantees them at least one to two free bags of clothing outfits at least once a month for everyone…at higher end retailer stores," said Franchesca with a noticeably nervous twitch that recently began on the right corner of her eye.

"ALL RIGHT," she bellowed out to the courtroom. "There is no Demuke, no after life of eternal bliss with our dark lord either. Actually, those people were so naïve to the point where we could have them all drink from the dark Lord's demonic water…even if it was piss and sugar water combined."

"What the hell?" asked the attorney incredulously. "Please do explain in full detail, Ms. Russo."

"Well, people with low self-esteem or no friends have no true sense of belonging. So, the congregation provides that for all of its loyal members. They were so loyal and sweet at first it was all very endearing. Then…we began to take advantage of their kindness and started to con all of the members out of a lot of money." She said with a crimson face of complete embarrassment.

"Would I assume this as a beginning to a true confession?" asked the attorney.

"Y- y- yes," stammered Franchesca with the most nervous mannerisms I had ever witnessed in my entire life.

"The only true reason that we murdered their parents was due to actually them confessing to us that they would talk with the authorities…so we had to put them down." She said without even the slightest remorse.

"Putting them down…isn't that what a veterinarian would accomplish towards an animal? Did they both mean that little to you people?" asked the attorney.

"Yes," confessed Franchesca and then she attempted the most horrific act of all. She just smiled and let out a laugh that emanated through the entire horrified courtroom.

"I cannot believe what I am hearing from her," I quietly muttered to Trevor.

My face was so crimson from the hate filled rage I had for Franchesca…I could not even control my temper.

Suddenly, I stood up, "Who the hell do you think you are? Just some two-bit crazy lady thinking that she can possibly get away with murder? You are one cold, ruthless, evil mother…."

"SILENCE!" bellowed the judge as he pounded his desk with the gavel.

"I want order in this courtroom immediately!!!" Then he gave a hard glare towards Franchesca and made his final statement.

"All right, I want a call to order right now!"

Silence suddenly filled the courtroom as if life had a remote control and god just decided to hit the pause button for just a moment.

Emanating laughter from Franchesca was later eliminated after the jury foreman read the final verdict: guilty on two charges of murder. Reality quickly hit Franchesca in the face…with her facial expression quickly turning into one of sheer terror. The hammer came down from Judge Haggard.

"The penalty will be death by means of the electrocution chair."

I felt for Franchesca's laughter to subside…our minds became a blur and then there was only an extremely insecure and nervous demeanor to remain as its replacement from Franchesca. The hammer came down again.

"Court is adjourned. All rise," bellowed the officer. Judge Haggard stomped off.

"Rex, are you enjoying this a bit TOO much?" Trevor asked me with some nervous tension protruding from his voice. Suddenly, I realized that my face was plastered with a unique smile. One smile that I never quite acquired after our parents died…until right at this exact moment in time. That is when I truly discovered that Lady Justice had taken her final say and fair legal justice was finally obtained for Trevor and myself, but more importantly, justice for our brutally murdered parents who had deserved to live a lot longer lives than they did. Like a moth to a flame, they fell for one of the biggest cons of all time…the trust of an absolute stranger. I felt as if a huge weight had been lifted off our shoulders. Maybe the end of this grim chapter would open up to reveal a much brighter new chapter in the end.

"So, said Trevor, want to go out and celebrate this victory for our folks?" he said with exuberant enthusiasm.

"Agreed" was all I could muster, "quick, Trevor, let's get out of here before I walk over to Franchesca and slap her back into reality," I said while quickly exiting out towards the courtroom.

"Reality bites" was the only snide remark that Trevor could muster back at the time.

Trevor silently followed me after that comment. Quickly realizing that it might actually happen if we were left here even a second more before the courtroom adjourned for the day.

"Agreed" was Trevor's only reply as we both quickly made our way out of the courtroom.

Later that night, we decided to go out to our parents' favorite restaurant to celebrate. Trevor ordered liver n' onions, dad's favorite. I ended up with some shrimp scampi on top of a bed of thickly cooked linguine, which was mom's favorite meal. We ate in silence at first then began later to reminisce about our parents. What we loved about them, what we hated about them, and every other little detail we could possibly remember about them, we actually took turns saying those memories aloud to each other.

After the meal, we both went back to our house and called it a night. Several minutes later, we each went into our own bedrooms and sleep took over the rest of our night. That much needed sleep where our nightmares and horrors just turned into fantastic epic dreams of pure victory. A victory over every demon that ever touched the sanctity of what we truly felt dear to our hearts: an unbroken family with loving parents that never truly died because they would reside within our fantastic dreams of cold justice…forever.

CHAPTER ELEVEN

Death Penalty

A call erupted right beside my right hand while I was watching television.

I let out a blood curdling scream that easily could have reached our own neighbors' ears. Quickly, I picked up the phone to figure out exactly who had called me. Over the receiver I heard those blissful words that put me right at ease.

"Franchesca and her brother receive the death penalty October 1st, at 2:00 p.m. of next year if we get this properly expedited. You are not required to be there, but you may attend behind the viewing panel with a few other selected individuals."

I numbly hung up the phone while the other person on the receiving end was still in mid-sentence. Calmly I walked into the kitchen where Trevor was preparing a meal for us. I picked up two different wire cords and tapped both to both sides of my temples around my forehead. A sadistic grin on my face finally announced,

"Anyone ready for some electro-shock therapy?" I said purposefully grinding my teeth in a crazed grin that almost put a shock to Trevor's nerves of steel like mannerism.

"No way," said Trevor in disbelief.

"Oh yeah, October 1st, they officially both get electrocuted."

"Well, I could have never in a million years predicted this turn of events Rex, it almost seems surreal," said Trevor as he looked at me with absolute disbelief very evident on his face.

"You're exactly right," I said in agreement as I made my way back into the living room to watch some more television.

"Who knows," I continued, "maybe these gruesome events will be on the media. Maybe we will have to defend ourselves if there is any slander thrown towards our parents over this entire chaos. Life sure is messy."

We were given a week's notice of the perpetrators' demise to better prepare ourselves in case we decided to witness the event of their electrocution. You better believe, after what they did to our parents, I would be there almost literally with bells and whistles on and a white shirt adorned with JUSTICE written on the front of it in a bold black Sharpie marker. Too bitter, you ask? Damn right!

On the actual day of Franchesca's and her brother's death penalty day I felt completely …hollow. Sure, there was the sweet revenge that they were finally receiving the death penalty. Then…to watch it happen to them? Have the same sadistic glee for their own demise that puts me down to their pathetic miscreant level? You better believe it!! I knew that I would relish every second of every moment for what happened to those perpetrators from their electrocution chair.

——— One Year Later… ———

When we arrived at the execution facility, we were bombarded by at least a dozen camera lenses straight at us.

"What the hell is going on?" asked the prosecuting attorney with authority in his voice. Realizing that we had all arrived, the attorney went on.

"Haven't these two been through enough?" He motioned silently with his hand to hold the cameras back for a moment. "Sorry media folks, wait until after the execution is done."

"Surely they will be in just the perfect mood to answer all of your manipulative questions for your prize-winning newspaper stories. The massive amounts of informative bullshit you provide to all your avid readers will be consumed at a later date and time. Now is not the time. Please wait until the execution has been officially completed."

Suddenly, a police officer stepped in front of the crowd of media on lookers to usher us into the building. Once inside, we all breathed a collective sigh of relief.

"Well, as long as there is suffering in this world, we will have the media around to report on it!" I said snottily.

"Agreed," was all my brother Trevor could muster up to say at that exact moment.

Trevor leaned in to me and grabbed my arm to usher me further into the building. Who knows what I would have done to the frenetic frenzy of media onlookers?

Trevor was following the officer who was cautiously leading the way towards where we would all be witnessing the execution. As we got closer, massive waves of nausea started within my lower intestines…or it may have been all because of the anticipation of seeing our sworn enemies finally arriving to their final demise. After my nausea subsided, we were again escorted towards where the execution was to begin.

Before opening the door, the officer quickly asked, "Are you sure you're ready for this?" He asked with legitimate concern strewn on his face.

"You better believe it, ready as I will ever be," I quickly said to the officer before Trevor could even put a word in edgewise.

Through some internal angry psychic energy that was exuded from Trevor's own pores, the officer finally got the clue to open the door for everyone.

"All right, but I must warn you both that what you are about to witness is going to be of a very graphic nature." Finally, he opened the door and quietly ushered us inside to take our seats.

After we took our front row seats, we both reconsidered our location. We hastily moved to the back row seats, just to remain on the safe side.

It seemed as if an hour passed, but it had only been ten minutes. Suddenly, five other members from Franchesca and her brother's congregation showed up as well. Eyes cast down, they all decided to not look at us DEAD in the eye…given the present situation.

Another ten minutes passed in silence between everyone in the room. After that, a middle-aged woman with her hair tied up in a proper bun entered the room. She walked in front of the first row of seats and then stood in front of everyone.

"In five minutes we will begin the execution of Franchesca Russo and her brother. We will please ask everyone to remain calm where they are seated and to make no further forms of communication until the actual execution has officially been performed." She sounded so calm when she talked she might as well have been talking about events so mundane such as the weather or traffic updates. Briskly, she walked out of the room and was mysteriously never seen or heard from ever again.

Five minutes later, an officer brought in Franchesca's brother. His overall haggard appearance was almost unbearable to witness. For the execution they had shaved his entire body, so he looked like some sort of overweight hairless cat ready for his own final demise. Facial features were a blank lake placid stare because now he knew it was down to the wire for his final last breath on this god forsaken earth. As they brought him close to the electric chair, a priest began to read him his last rites before the end of his own final fate. Towards the end of the reading of his rites, he began to fight against the officer that was currently restraining him. He looked as if he might resist the officer and break free, but with a fierce twist of the arm from the officer that was a true end to the possibility of an even more chaotic beginning.

Finally, the officer unlatched the handcuffs off of him and quickly proceeded to place him into the electric chair. After that, the officer briskly left the room and allowed the two people proceeding with the actual execution to officially take over. One person had the duty of tying his wrists with the heavy brown leather straps to keep his body in place for when the first initial electric shocks would begin. Another person had the duty of tying his ankles to the chair. The initial first shock waves to the body are unknown as to how each body will specifically act towards it. After that was accomplished, they carefully put a specially made bag over his head so as not to see the gruesome sight of the defendant's eyes almost popping out of their sockets. No matter how evil the two perpetrators may obviously be, some gruesome sights should be left hidden for only god to make his final judgment call.

Now, a final check is performed by both people that strapped him into the electric chair. To ensure that there are no surprises, they decide to be meticulous about their procedure for securing Franchesca's brother to the chair. Examples of possible problems such as flying out of the seat due to initial shock or the small possibility of trying to escape while they are still only half way alive and already having convulsions. Not that they had ever experienced this through previous perpetrators…well…we can leave it to your own imagination why they are NOW required to be more meticulous.

With everything double checked and in its proper place, the two executioners stood back for a moment. Suddenly, Franchesca's brother gives a final desperate pull for his last chance at life. Violently tugging and pulling against his restraints that viciously bound him to the chair, the two executioners stood back in shock…seriously…where the hell would he go? A nice trip to Cancun? Or possibly Jamaica? He knew the end of his life was here, but damn if he would actually accept it. After five minutes of viciously struggling against the restraints, he finally slumped over in a very defeatist position as if to physically say, hey, this is it, this is the end of my own demise and I finally choose to accept it.

After making sure that he would not struggle again, he still remained slumped over in a very defeatist position. So, without any further hesitation, one of the executioners flipped the switch. Racing currents of electricity pulsed through his veins, like sending lightning intravenously through your body with a syringe needle.

Bolting from his chair was not an option, so he literally just looked like some type of filthy worm writhing in his own pile of dirt. Smoke fumes began signaling precariously out of his head covering, so we all knew that his own demise was drawing towards a close. Suddenly, the second executioner hit the switch for the second wave of electrocution. Waves of nauseating and searing mini bolts of lightning intravenously swam through his veins. Every spare inch of his body began to convulse, as if he were having a seizure. Cardiac arrest followed, and all that remained was just a lifeless body in place for the strong man that he used to be while alive. Now dead, he seemed actually more pathetic than scary. Just some two-bit bastard that rightfully got what he truly deserved…COLD JUSTICE.

Next, the two executioners stood back to assess the actual time of death. Another jotted down a few notes, probably for "future" educational institutions for a police academy that resided nearby.

Trevor leaned into me and grabbed my arm to whisper, "Well, one down…One more to go!!" He said while glaring at the lifeless body of Franchesca's brother.

I merely stared at the man's lifeless body and thought to myself...I really wish that was Franchesca!!

The other executioner attempted to remove the cloth bag that hid the individual's face.... The entire viewing panel was covered in a pure black opaque abyss as the other executioner had recently put up a single gigantic black cloth covering to quickly hide the gruesome face of the perpetrator's own final demise.

It seemed as if time itself stood still as we waited for the next individual to make their way into the electric chair and then have their demise finally finalized.

The gruesome sound of the clock ticking away seemed to take nearly a small portion of my very own soul away with it. When the hell was Franchesca going to make her appearance? It was a beautiful trip down memory lane just remembering her during the trial...obviously this is complete sarcasm on my part.

Anyways, the moment of truth had finally arrived for Trevor and myself. One of the executioners led Franchesca into the room and ushered her quickly towards the electric chair. Showing no remorse, which was her custom, she decided to make a lewd gesture towards the on lookers. By giving us all the middle finger through the panel.

Fucking Bitch.

Shuffling along with her head held in an almost defeatist position, it looked as though Franchesca had just given up her own will to live in just a few seconds. Suddenly, out of nowhere, she viciously turned on the unsuspecting executioner and sunk her teeth deep into the flesh of the unknowing right side of his cheek.

Screaming in agonizing pain, the executioner viciously shoved Franchesca into the electric chair and then hand motioned the other executioner to begin the process of tying the straps down on Franchesca for strict security purposes.

"You will NEVER get away with this...I deserve better treatment... an overall better life!!!" Screamed Franchesca at the top of her lungs.

"Really? Well, I deserve to have my face still attached to my body... that's MY overall better life!!!!" Roared the other executioner in an absolute white rage.

Before anything else could further occur, Franchesca was finally strapped down to the chair and then quickly was given some type of sedative to tone her emotions down a bit. After a few moments, she began to calm down and now was slightly slumped in the chair with a dead pan lake placid look permanently taking complete control of her facial features.

Next, the same executioner that strapped her to the chair also decided to put the canvas bag over her head just in case anything dire may happen during electrocution.

The moment of truth was upon us...but how would I truly feel with the aftermath of it all? I would soon find out myself in just a few moments...

Suddenly, the two executioners talked amongst themselves for a moment. The injured one was gently cleaning his wound with some type of antiseptic wipe that he brought out from his pocket. Finally, the one closest to the actual switch turned it on in high anticipation for the upcoming event.

Currents of electricity pulsed through Franchesca's veins as the first initial jolt was administered. Nervous tension was now finally gone from my body. Still, the initial first shock did not seem to have any effect on Franchesca. Still, the second wave of electrocution seemed to do the trick. Reeling back from her seat in the chair, her head was thrown back as if looking up towards the heavens...would God even give a final chance for her...

Probably not!!!

Finally, her minor shakes and tremors led to a series of massive convulsions within her body that looked extremely difficult to watch. Smoke rings circled out where her head was covered. Before she was set on fire, she finally convulsed one more time to escape her chair.. only to die in it the very next moment. Franchesca was now nothing more than a mere nightmare that we all finally woke up from with the sweetest relief that it was finally over. Franchesca was now finally dead...my nightmare just finally turned into a restful and peaceful sleep in heaven.

That hateful bitch was finally dead...now that's some Cold Justice!!!!!!!